This book belongs to

. . . .

LADYBIRD BOOKS
UK | USA | Canada | Ireland | Australia
India | New Zealand | South Africa

Ladybird Books is part of the Penguin Random House group of companies
whose addresses can be found at global.penguinrandomhouse.com.

ladybird.com

First published 2016
006

This book is based on the TV series *Peppa Pig*
Peppa Pig is created by Neville Astley and Mark Baker

www.peppapig.com

Printed in China

A CIP catalogue record for this book is available from the British Library

ISBN: 978-0-241-24519-4

Peppa and her Golden Boots

It was the day of the Big Puddle-Jumping Competition. Peppa and her friends were practising jumping up and down in muddy puddles.

Hee! Hee!

"My daddy **always** wins," boasted Peppa. "He says the first rule of puddle-jumping is to wear your boots. And mine are very special because they are made of gold!"

Hee! Hee!

"They are **not** gold," replied Suzy Sheep. "They're yellow."

"They are not yellow. They are real plastic **gold**!" protested Peppa.

"Would anyone like some orange juice?"
called Mummy Pig from the house.
"Yes, please!" replied everyone.
They ran inside, leaving their
boots outside the front door.

When Peppa and her friends had finished their juice, they headed outside to put on their boots.
"Oh no! My boots have gone!" sobbed Peppa.

Mr Zebra arrived with the post.
"I've just seen a duck with boots on!" he said.
Peppa sniffed. "Were they gold?"
"No – yellow," he replied.

Mrs Duck came running down the hill wearing Peppa's golden boots! Peppa ran after her. "Mrs Duck! Can I have my boots back, please?"

But Mrs Duck did not want to give Peppa's boots back.
She didn't stop running until she reached Captain Dog's boat.

No one could stop Mrs Duck! She leapt into the water and swam away.
Captain Dog started his engine. "I think my boat can go faster than that duck!" he exclaimed.
But Captain Dog's boat could not keep up with Mrs Duck.
"Hmmm, that's a fast duck," he said.

Mrs Duck finally stopped at a little island, where Grampy Rabbit had been shipwrecked when his boat capsized.

"Mrs Duck has my boots and she won't give them back!" Peppa called.

"Don't worry, Peppa!" replied Grampy Rabbit. "Mrs Duck has nowhere to go!"

But then Mrs Duck started flying – and she was still wearing the boots!

“Oh no!” cried Peppa. “Mrs Duck is flying to the moon with my boots!” “Don’t worry, Peppa,” said Grampy Rabbit, pointing to the neighbouring island. “We’ll take my rocket!”

“Er, I really don’t think Peppa’s boots will be on the moon . . .” said Mummy Pig.

"Nonsense!" insisted Grampy Rabbit, helping everyone into the rocket.

Five . . . four . . . three . . . two . . . one . . .

BLAST OFF!

On the moon, Peppa and her friends searched everywhere for Mrs Duck and the golden boots.
"Let's ask at the shop!" suggested Suzy Sheep.
"You don't get shops on the moon!" exclaimed Daddy Pig.

"Postcards!" called Miss Rabbit
from inside her gift shop. "Ice cream!
Buckets and spades!"

Meanwhile, Grandpa Pig had spotted Mrs Duck in his garden.
“Those aren’t your boots, are they?” he asked.
He quickly dialled Daddy Pig’s number . . .

"Hello, Grandpa Pig," said Daddy Pig.
"Yes, Peppa **has** lost some boots.
We'll be right there!"
"Next stop, Grandpa Pig's garden!"
announced Grampy Rabbit.

Peppa bounced excitedly out of the rocket.
"My boots, my golden boots!" she exclaimed.
"Thank you, Grandpa!"
Grandpa Pig helped Peppa put them on.
"Now we can go to the puddle-jumping
competition!" said Mummy Pig.
"Oh yes!" agreed Daddy Pig.
"We'd better hurry!"

The Big Puddle-Jumping Competition was about to begin.
"First up . . . Daddy Pig!" cried Mr Potato.

Daddy Pig took a giant leap . . .

and made a very BIG splash!

Then it was Mr Elephant's turn . . . and Mr Elephant
made an even BIGGER splash!
"Mr Elephant is the winner!" announced Mr Potato.

Peppa cleared her throat.
"Please can I have a go, too?" she asked.
"Oh, of course!" replied Mr Potato.
"And can all my friends help?" Peppa added.

Mr Elephant was not pleased.
"Um, hang on. I don't think that's really –"
"It sounds perfectly fair to me," interrupted Daddy Pig.

Peppa and her friends formed a circle and held hands.

"Five . . .

four . . .

three . . .

two . . .

one!"

they all chanted.

"JUMP!"

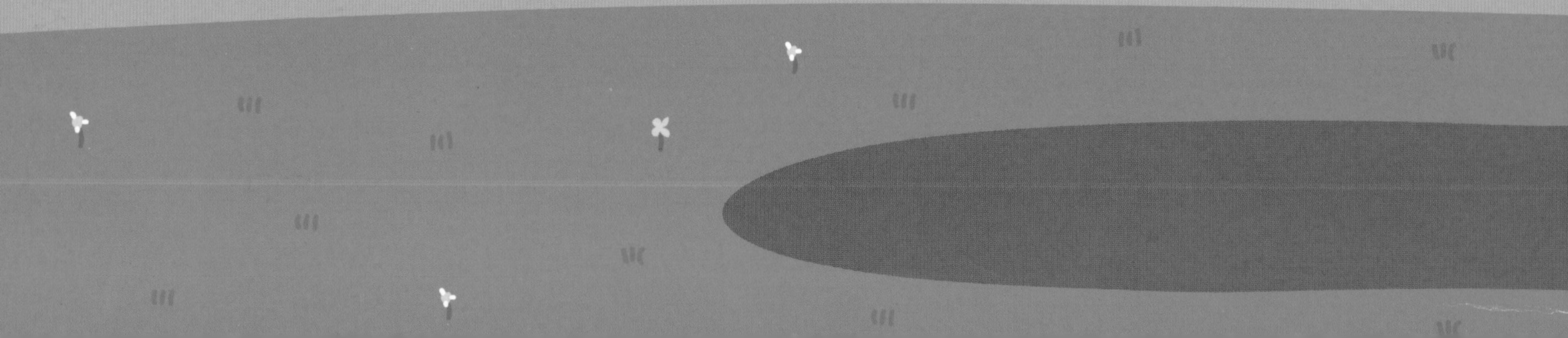

Wheeeeee!

Peppa and her friends made the biggest splash ever!
"Peppa and her friends are the winners!" declared Mr Potato.

"Um, I still think –" began Mr Elephant.
"Hooray!" cheered everyone, loudly.

Peppa loved her golden boots.
Everyone loved their boots.
And everyone loved the Big Puddle-Jumping Competition!